When Daddy Comes Home

Story by Linda Wagner Tyler
Pictures by Susan Davis

Viking Kestrel

VIKING KESTREL

Viking Penguin Inc., 40 West 23rd Street, New York, New York 10010, U.S.A.
Penguin Books Ltd, Harmondsworth, Middlesex, England
Penguin Books Australia Ltd, Ringwood, Victoria, Australia
Penguin Books Canada Limited, 2801 John Street, Markham, Ontario, Canada L3R 1B4
Penguin Books (N.Z.) Ltd, 182-190 Wairau Road, Auckland 10, New Zealand

Text copyright © Linda Tyler, 1986
Illustrations copyright © Susan Davis, 1986
All rights reserved

First published in 1986 by Viking Penguin Inc.
Published simultaneously in Canada
Printed in Japan by Dai Nippon.
Set in Souvenir Light
1   2   3   4   5   90   89   88   87   86

Library of Congress Cataloging in Publication Data
Tyler, Linda.   When daddy comes home.
Summary: A young hippo is delighted when his father,
who doesn't usually get home until his son is asleep,
decides to set aside a special day every week for the
two of them to work together on special projects.
[1. Fathers and sons—Fiction.   2. Hippopotamus—
Fiction]   I. Davis, Susan,   ill.   II. Title.
PZ7.T94Wh   1986   [E]   85-31459   ISBN 0-670-80301-4

For my husband Patrick and our children Silas and Landry
with special thanks for this story. And to Lynne Perri. — L.W.T.

For my Dad with love. — S.D.

My Dad comes home every night after I am asleep.

That's because he writes a story every day
for the morning newspaper.

He has to wait while someone called an Editor
reads it.

The story must be ready at 8 o'clock.

My bedtime.

My friend Tucky is lucky. His Dad comes home every night at 6 and they read and talk together.

I asked Mom if I could stay up until Dad came home
so we could do things together, too.

She said not every night, but we could plan
to have special evenings.

Dad promised to come home at 7 o'clock
the very next night.

He said we would work on an exciting project.

And he told me to be sure to take my bath
and brush my teeth before he got home.

That night I was so excited I ate my dinner
very fast.

I put out my clothes for the morning in case
we stayed up late.

When Dad came home, he was carrying a
crystal radio kit.

He explained how it picks up invisible sound waves.

We worked very hard to put it together.

I told Dad about my day in school.

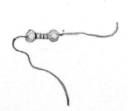

Dad talked about the City Hall story he is writing.

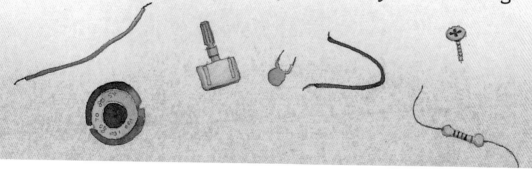

When we were finished we taped a green wire
to the window.

I listened to the sound waves coming through.

On the way up to bed, I said to Dad,

"Thanks for the radio," and gave him a hug.

Dad said, "I can't wait for the next project."

We listened to the weather report.

"The forecast for tomorrow is sunny and warm."

The next day Tucky wanted to see the radio
Dad and I built.

He listened to the sports report.

I showed him the instructions. "Wow!" Tucky said.
"I wish *my* Dad knew how to make things like this."

"But Tucky," I said, "your Dad tells great stories—like the one about Paul Revere."

I guess all Dads are good at different things.

And it's fun for us...

to share them.